Merry Christmas, WITHDRAWN
Dear Dragon

by Margaret Hillert
Illustrated by Carl Kock

NORWOOD HOUSE 🏠 PRESS

DEAR CAREGIVER,

The *Beginning-to-Read* series is a carefully written collection of classic readers you may remember from your own childhood. Each book features text comprised of common sight words to provide your child ample practice reading the words that appear most frequently in written text. The many additional details in the pictures enhance the story and offer the opportunity for you to help your child expand oral language and develop comprehension.

Begin by reading the story to your child, followed by letting him or her read familiar words and soon your child will be able to read the story independently. At each step of the way, be sure to praise your reader's efforts to build his or her confidence as an independent reader. Discuss the pictures and encourage your child to make connections between the story and his or her own life. At the end of the story, you will find reading activities and a word list that will help your child practice and strengthen beginning reading skills.

Above all, the most important part of the reading experience is to have fun and enjoy it!

Shannon Cannon

Shannon Cannon,
Literacy Consultant

Norwood House Press • P.O. Box 316598 • Chicago, Illinois 60631
For more information about Norwood House Press please visit our website at *www.norwoodhousepress.com* or call 866-565-2900.

LIBRARY OF CONGRESS CATALOGING-IN-PUBLICATION DATA
Hillert, Margaret.
   Merry Christmas, dear dragon / by Margaret Hillert; illustrated
by Carl Kock. — Rev. and expanded library ed.
     p. cm. — (Beginning to read series. Dear dragon)
   Summary: A boy and his pet dragon share many winter activities
and celebrate Christmas by chopping down and decorating a tree,
making cookies, and sitting by a fire. Includes reading activities.
   ISBN-13: 978-1-59953-042-0 (library binding : alk. paper)
   ISBN-10: 1-59953-042-2 (library binding : alk. paper)
   [1. Winter—Fiction. 2. Christmas—Fiction. 3. Dragons—Fiction.]
I. Kock, Carl, ill. II. Title. III. Series.
PZ7.H558Me 2007
[E]—dc22
                         2006007091

Look at this.
Down, down it comes.
What fun.
What fun.

But it is work, too.
I will have to work.
I can make it go away.

Oh, my.
Look at you.
You can help me.
What a big help you are.

We can play, too.
It is fun to play in this.
Run, run, run.
And jump, jump, jump.

We can make something big.
Big, big, big.
See, see.
It looks like you!

Oh, oh.
Look at that car.
It can not go.

You can help.
Work, work, work.
Now it can go away.
That is good.

Now come with me.
We have to get something.
Something for the house.

Look here. Look here.
Here is the one we want.
Not too little.
Not too big.

13

Mother. Mother.
See me ride.
Look what we have.
It is for the house.

I see it.
I like it.
It is a good one.
Come in. Come in.

See what we can make.
Cookies. Cookies.
Look at this —
    and this —
       and this.

One for me.
And one for you.
A big, big one for you!

Now we will do this.
Here are some balls.
This is fun.
I like to do this.

You can help with this one.
Make it go up.
Up, up, up.

Where are you now?
Where did you go?
I can not guess.
I can not find you.

Come here.
Come here.
I want you.
I like you here with me.

Oh, here you are!
I see you now.
Look at you.
You are funny.

24

Here is something.
I can not make it work.
You will have to do it for me.

Oh, my. Oh, my.
Look at it now.
Red and yellow.
I like this.

Here you are with me.
And here I am with you.
Oh, what a merry Christmas, dear dragon.

The following activities support the findings of the National Reading Panel that determined the most effective components for reading instruction are: Phonemic Awareness, Phonics, Vocabulary, Fluency, and Text Comprehension.

Phonemic Awareness: The /m/ sound

Oddity Task: Say the /**m**/ sound for your child. Read each word below to your child and ask your child to say the word without the /**m**/ sound:

mad - /m/ = ad	moat - /m/ = oat	mice - /m/ = ice
man - /m/ = an	mend - /m/ = end	mill - /m/ = ill
meat - /m/ = eat	mat - /m/ = at	

Phonics: The letter Mm

1. Demonstrate how to form the letters **M** and **m** for your child.
2. Have your child practice writing **M** and **m** at least three times each.
3. Ask your child to point to the words in the book that begin with the letter **m**.
4. Write down the following words and ask your child to circle the letter **m** in each word:

merry	make	yam	comb	my	jam
mother	moon	farm	me	tummy	from
tumble	room	make	map	camp	mom

Vocabulary: Concept Words

1. Fold a piece of paper vertically in half.
2. Draw a line down the fold to divide the paper in two parts.
3. Write the words **work** and **play** in separate columns at the top of the page.
4. Write the following statements on separate pieces of paper:

shoveling snow	riding a sled	building a snowman
baking cookies	cleaning house	emptying the garbage
watching movies	using the computer	picking up toy
raking leaves	walking a dog	washing dishes

5. Read each statement aloud and ask your child whether the action belongs in the **work** or **play** column. (Note: some may be considered work and play, depending on the situation.)

6. Invite your child to tell you why he or she has chosen the column.

Fluency: Choral Reading

1. Reread the story with your child at least two more times while your child tracks the print by running a finger under the words as they are read. Ask your child to read the words he or she knows with you.

2. Reread the story aloud together. Be careful to read at a rate that your child can keep up with.

3. Repeat choral reading and allow your child to be the lead reader and ask him or her to change from a whisper to a loud voice while you follow along and change your voice.

Text Comprehension: Discussion Time

1. Ask your child to retell the sequence of events in the story.

2. To check comprehension, ask your child the following questions:

  • How did Dear Dragon help the boy and his family?
  • Why couldn't the car go on page 9?
  • Why does the boy look sad on pages 22-23?
  • What is your favorite part of the story? Why?
  • What are some of the things your family does to celebrate Christmas?

(If your family celebrates another winter holiday, substitute that holiday for Christmas)

WORD LIST

***Merry Christmas, Dear Dragon* uses the 69 words listed below.**
This list can be used to practice reading the words that appear in the text. You may wish to write the words on index cards and use them to help your child build automatic word recognition. Regular practice with these words will enhance your child's fluency in reading connected text.

a	dear	have	make	see
am	did	help	me	something
and	do	here	merry	
are	down	house	mother	that
at	dragon		my	the
away		I		this
	father	in	not	to
balls	find	is	now	too
big	for	it		
but	fun		oh	want
	funny	jump	one	we
can				what
car	get	like	play	where
Christmas	go	little		will
come(s)	good	look(s)	red	with
cookies	guess		ride	work
			run	
				yellow
				you

ABOUT THE AUTHOR Margaret Hillert has written over 80 books for children who are just learning to read. Her books have been translated into many different languages and over a million children throughout the world have read her books. She first started writing poetry as a child and has continued to write for children and adults throughout her life. A first grade teacher for 34 years, Margaret is now retired from teaching and lives in Michigan where she likes to write, take walks in the morning, and care for her three cats.

Photograph by Glenna Washburn

ABOUT THE ADVISER Shannon Cannon contributed the activities pages that appear in this book. Shannon serves as a literacy consultant and provides staff development to help improve reading instruction. She is a frequent presenter at educational conferences and workshops. Prior to this she worked as an elementary school teacher and as president of a curriculum publishing company.